D0529296

Contents

THE CREATIVE IMPULSE

M rs Albert Forrester was fifty-seven years old when she wrote her best-selling book, *The Achilles Statue*. This book was a great success. The critics[1] praised *The Achilles Statue* because they thought it was a great work of literature. More important for Mrs Albert Forrester, the public[1] bought the book in large quantities. As soon as the book arrived in bookshops in England and America, people hurried to buy it.

Mrs Albert Forrester became a very rich woman. In fact, she made enough money from this one book to live comfortably for the rest of her life.

Before she wrote *The Achilles Statue*, Mrs Albert Forrester had written many other books. Her first book was a book of poems and she wrote that when she was only eighteen years old. And every three or four years after that, another book appeared with her name on it.

By the time she was fifty-seven, Mrs Albert Forrester had written half a dozen[5] books of poetry, half a dozen books of essays and half a dozen other books, all of them very serious and learned[1]. All of these books had been highly praised by the critics. All the critics agreed that Mrs Albert Forrester's books were excellent. She was considered by the critics to be a writer of the highest merit[1].

But critics do not buy books. It is the public who buy books. And the public thought that Mrs Albert Forrester's books were dull and uninteresting. They did not buy them.

All that changed suddenly when she wrote *The Achilles Statue*. The critics praised it and the public bought it. Mrs Albert Forrester's life changed completely. But how, at the age of fifty-seven, did Mrs Albert Forrester come to write this remarkable best seller? What experience in a writer's life makes him or her write a particular book? What experience in her life – what *creative impulse* – made Mrs Albert Forrester write this best-selling detective story?

———

Mrs Albert Forrester lived with her husband in a flat not far from Marble Arch. Marble Arch was very near to the most fashionable[2] part of London.

At the front of the flat, facing the street, there was a handsome drawing-room[2] and a large bedroom for Mrs Albert Forrester. At the back of the flat there was a dark dining-room and a dark kitchen. Next to the kitchen, there was a tiny bedroom for the man who paid the rent of the flat, Mr Albert Forrester – her husband.

Every Tuesday afternoon, many visitors came to have tea with Mrs Albert Forrester in her handsome drawing-room. It was a handsome room, but it was not very comfortable. In the brightest corner of the room stood the desk at which Mrs Albert Forrester sat and wrote the books which the critics praised but the public did not buy.

Mrs Albert Forrester was a very large lady. Luckily, she was also very tall so that she did not appear to be fat. Her face was large and this made her look very intelligent. Her eyes were large and black and bright. Her nose was large and her chin was square. She looked very important.

Because she looked so important, Mrs Albert Forrester did not serve[2] the tea herself. Tea was served by Miss Warren. It was not easy to guess Miss Warren's age, but she certainly did not look at all important. She never said a word and she was never introduced to anyone.

The visitors who came to tea all believed that Miss Warren enjoyed serving tea at Mrs Albert Forrester's tea-parties.

Mrs Albert Forrester believed that conversation was very important. She herself was an excellent talker on all kinds of subjects. But her conversation was always serious. No one had ever heard Mrs Albert Forrester tell a joke.

Mrs Albert Forrester was a well-read lady. She had read all the books that everyone else had read. And she had a good memory. She was able to quote[1] passages from the books she had read. People who are able to quote from books are often thought to be lively, bright and intelligent.

All kinds of people came to her Tuesday afternoon tea-parties – politicians, owners of newspapers, foreign ambassadors. But her favourite visitors were writers – especially if they were not known. She was always ready to offer advice and give encouragement to unknown writers who, one day, might become famous.

Mrs Albert Forrester had helped many writers who had later become famous. Some of these writers had made a lot of money from their writing. Mrs Albert Forrester was never able to do this, but the good lady did not show any signs of envy[3]. She did not worry about making money from her writing. She seemed quite satisfied to be a writer of the highest literary merit.

Her Tuesday afternoon tea-parties were famous. Everyone who was invited to one of Mrs Albert Forrester's tea-parties felt that they had been honoured[2]. They had to sit on the rather uncomfortable chairs, but they felt that they were taking part in something very important.

Mr Albert Forrester was never present at these afternoon tea-parties. He was too busy at work in his office in the City[5]. But he was always present at Mrs Albert Forrester's weekly lunch-parties, which were held every Saturday. The conversation at these lunch-parties was always interesting and the food and the wine were always excellent. It was an honour to be invited to one of her Tuesday tea-parties. It was an even greater honour to be invited to one of her Saturday lunches.

The guests at her Saturday lunches always praised the food.

But Mrs Albert Forrester never allowed them to praise her.

'Please do not praise me,' she would say. 'Praise Mrs Bulfinch.'

'Who is Mrs Bulfinch?' the guests would ask.

'Mrs Bulfinch is my cook,' Mrs Albert Forrester would reply.

But if anyone praised the cigars, Mrs Albert Forrester would smile happily.

'If you are pleased with the cigars, you must praise Albert. It is Albert who chooses the cigars. No one knows more about a cigar than Albert.'

She would look at her husband proudly. He would make a pleasant reply to the visitor who had praised the cigars.

'You are very kind,' he would say.

Then Albert would give a little talk about cigars and how to choose them. Mrs Forrester always listened carefully to what he had to say. And all the other guests listened carefully too. Albert's little talk was always a great success. But you cannot go on talking about cigars for ever. So, after a time, Mrs Albert Forrester would change the subject of the conversation and the guests would start talking about other things. Albert would sit back in silence once again. But he had had his moment of success.

Apart from his little talk about cigars, he never said anything. It was almost as if he was not there at all.

But Mr Albert Forrester was always there when Mrs Albert Forrester wanted him. And he was not there when he was not wanted. Mrs Albert Forrester did not allow her guests to make fun of him. She was always the first to praise him and say what a good husband he was.

'I really don't know what I would do without him,' she often said.

Her visitors thought that it was very kind of her to praise such a dull and uninteresting husband. If he had been a wealthy man, it would be easy to understand why she was so fond of him. But Mr Albert Forrester was not wealthy. He was only a currant merchant[5] and did not make much money at all. He made just enough money to enable Mrs Albert Forrester to hold her weekly tea-parties and her weekly Saturday lunch-parties.

It was near the end of one of Mrs Albert Forrester's tea-parties, however, that Mr Albert Forrester showed that he was not always dull.

It had been one of her most successful tea-parties. The Leader of the Labour Party had been there. The American Ambassador had been there and also a Russian prince.

It was late in the afternoon when the important event happened. By that time, most of her visitors had left. A few still remained: Clifford Boylestone, Harry Oakland, Rose Waterford, Oscar Charles and Simmons. The first three were writers, but not very important writers, and Simmons was her publisher.

Oscar Charles was a critic. He wrote articles in the newspapers in which he criticised other people's writings. He was often cruel in his criticism. But he was never cruel to Mrs Albert Forrester. He always praised her writings. She respected[3] him and liked his praise; but she was, at the same time, rather afraid of him and of what he might write.

Simmons looked after the business of publishing Mrs Albert Forrester's writings. He was round-faced and wore thick glasses. He came regularly to the Tuesday afternoon tea-parties.

These remaining guests were sitting in a circle round Mrs Albert Forrester, discussing the visitors who had been present that afternoon. And they were not discussing them kindly.

Miss Warren, the silent lady who poured out the tea, was there too. She was busy clearing away the dirty teacups and dirty plates. Miss Warren had a job but she was always able to come to Mrs Albert Forrester's tea-parties.

Suddenly there was a loud crashing noise. It came from just outside the door of the drawing-room. The loud crashing noise was followed by angry voices. Mrs Albert Forrester frowned[3] angrily.

'What is going on?' she asked. 'Miss Warren would you please ring the bell for the maid and ask her what is the meaning of this noise.'

Miss Warren rang the bell and a few moments later the maid appeared. Miss Warren spoke to her quietly, asking her what was going on. But Mrs Albert Forrester interrupted her and spoke to the maid in a loud voice.

'What is going on? What is the reason for that dreadful noise? Is the house falling down?'

'I'm sorry, ma'am,' replied the maid. 'It's the new cook's box. The porter[2] dropped it as he was carrying it through the door and the cook got angry.'

'New cook? What do you mean?'

'Mrs Bulfinch went away this afternoon,' replied the maid.

Mrs Albert Forrester stared at the maid in amazement.

'This is the first I have heard about this. When did Mrs Bulfinch leave? Tell Mr Forrester the moment he comes in that I wish to speak to him.'

The maid left the room and Miss Warren returned to the tea-table. She poured out some cups of tea, though nobody wanted to drink them.

'What a disaster!' cried Miss Waterford.

'You must get her back,' said Clifford Boylestone.

'She is the best cook in London.'

At that moment, the maid came back into the room. She was carrying a letter on a small silver tray.

'What is this?' asked Mrs Albert Forrester.

'A letter,' replied the maid. 'Mr Albert Forrester said I was to give it to you when you asked for him.'

'Where is Mr Forrester?'

'Mr Forrester's gone,' replied the maid. 'He left this morning. Didn't you know?'

Mrs Albert Forrester looked surprised.

'Thank you. You can go,' she said to the maid. There was a puzzled look on her face as she opened the letter and began to read it. The puzzled look on her face turned to a look of complete amazement.

'Monstrous!' she cried. 'Monstrous! Monstrous!'

'What is it, Mrs Forrester?' the guests asked.

'Albert has eloped[4] with the cook!'

There were gasps of dismay[3] from the guests. Then something terrible happened. Miss Warren, who was standing behind the tea-table, suddenly laughed. Miss Warren, who never spoke and who no one ever spoke to, suddenly burst out into loud laughter. The guests turned and gazed at Miss Warren. She tried to stop her laughter by stuffing a handkerchief into her mouth. But she could not stop laughing. With one last howl of laughter, she turned and ran from the room.

'Shock. She is laughing because she is shocked,' said Clifford Boylestone.

But Mrs Albert Forrester said nothing. The letter fell from her hand and dropped at her feet. Simmons picked it up and handed it to her. But she would not take it.

'Read it,' she said to Simmons. 'Read it aloud.'

My Dear,

Mrs Bulfinch needs a rest and a change in her life and has decided to leave. I do not feel like staying on here without her so I am leaving too. I have had enough talk about literature to last me for the rest of my life.

Mrs Bulfinch does not mind if we do not get married. But if you are ready to divorce[4] me, she is ready to marry me. I hope you find the new cook satisfactory. She has excellent references[2]. Mrs Bulfinch and I are going to live at 411, Kennington Road, South East London.

Albert

There was silence in the room. Everyone felt embarrassed[3]. Then Rose Waterford spoke.

She tried to stop her laughter by stuffing a handkerchief into her mouth.

'What does Mrs Bulfinch look like?' she asked.

'How should I know?' replied Mrs Albert Forrester. 'I hardly ever saw her. Albert looked after the servants. I left it all to him. He did it all so that I could get on with my writing.'

'What about the Saturday lunches?' asked Clifford Boylestone. 'Did Albert take care of those too?'

'Of course. That was his responsibility.'

Clifford Boylestone remembered all the good food he had eaten. What a fool he had been never to guess that it had all been Albert's work.

'I always told you how much he did for me,' went on Mrs Forrester. 'But you would not believe me.'

There was no answer to this and once again the room became silent. Suddenly Mr Simmons shocked them all with his next words.

'You must get him back.'

'What do you mean?' cried Mrs Albert Forrester. 'I refuse to see him again as long as I live. Take him back? Never!'

'I did not say take him back[4]. I said get him back.'

'Never! I'll never take him back,' repeated Mrs Albert Forrester angrily, ignoring Mr Simmons' interruption.

But her anger had no effect on Mr Simmons.

'How are you going to live? Where is the money going to come from?' he asked quietly.

'God will provide,' she answered coldly.

'How much money do you think Mr Forrester makes in the currant business?' asked Mr Simmons.

'Very little,' replied Mrs Albert Forrester with a sigh. 'About twelve hundred pounds a year.'

'He must spend the money very wisely,' went on Mr Simmons. 'Your tea-parties and lunch-parties must cost a lot of money. And now that he has left you and is living in Kennington Road, he will not be able to give you as much as before. Believe me, there is only one thing for you to do – you must get him back.'

'I prefer to live in poverty[5]. How can I fight with a cook for the love of my husband? It's ridiculous.'

'That is exactly what it is – ridiculous. And that's my point. People will laugh at you. And that is the last thing you want. It will destroy your reputation[2]. You will become a joke.'

Mrs Albert Forrester looked at Simmons carefully. She was beginning to understand what he was saying.

'Explain what you mean,' she said.

'If your husband had run away with a beautiful young woman, it would not have been so terrible. People would have thought it a beautiful romance. But your husband has run away with your cook and everyone will laugh at you. In one week, all of London society[2] will be laughing at you. You will be a joke and that will be the end of your literary reputation. That's why you must get your husband back. And you must do it quickly.'

An angry look appeared on Mrs Albert Forrester's face, but she did not reply immediately. She was thinking about Miss Warren's loud laughter – laughter that had made Miss Warren run from the room.

'We are all friends here,' went on Mr Simmons. 'I am sure none of us will spread this story. But you must do something quickly before people find out what has happened.'

Mrs Albert Forrester looked round the room. She looked at Oscar Charles and remembered the cruel things he had written about other writers. She realised that, apart from Simmons, she could not trust any of them. She was sorry now that she had asked Simmons to read the letter aloud.

But Mr Simmons was a clever man. He knew what writers and critics were like.

'And we are all in trouble too,' he went on, looking slowly round the room at everyone present. 'Whatever happens to Mrs Albert Forrester affects us all here. We come here every Tuesday – and we often come here for lunch on Saturday. When people laugh at Mrs Albert Forrester, they will be laughing at us too. The fact is that Mr Albert Forrester has made us all look fools.'

'I agree,' said Clifford Boylestone. 'We will all be affected by this scandal[2]. It will destroy our reputations. You must do something, Mrs Forrester.'

'But what am I to do?'

Mr Simmons was a practical man.

'Mrs Forrester,' he said, 'you must go and see him tomorrow. We have his address in this letter. You must go and see him and beg him to come back.'

They all sat in silence and looked at Mrs Albert Forrrester.

'Will you do it?' asked Rose Waterford quietly.

Mrs Albert Forrester turned away from them and looked at the fireplace. There was a long silence. At last she spoke.

'I will do it,' she said. 'I must do it not for myself, but for my friends. I do not want you all to look fools. Yes, I will go and see him tomorrow.'

'Excellent,' said Mr Simmons. 'I will call here tomorrow afternoon on my way home from work. I hope to find you and Mr Forrester happily together again.'

He got up and the others stood up quickly. None of them wanted to be left alone with Mrs Albert Forrester.

———

On the following afternoon, Mrs Albert Forrester took a bus from Marble Arch to Victoria Station. Mr Simmons, being a practical man, told her the cheapest way to get to Kennington Road. At Victoria Station, she got on a tram[5].

When the tram crossed the River Thames, Mrs Albert Forrester found herself in a part of London she did not know. It was much more crowded and much noisier than where she lived. When she got off the tram in Kennington Road, she felt quite lost. She felt like a stranger in a foreign city.

She found house number four hundred and eleven. It was a shabby[5] house. The door was opened by a badly-dressed young girl.

'Does Mrs Bulfinch live here?' asked Mrs Albert Forrester in a quiet voice.

'Upstairs,' replied the girl, pointing to the stairway and at the same time shouting loudly: 'Someone to see you, Mrs Bulfinch.'

Mrs Forrester walked up the shabby stairs which were covered with a torn carpet. A door opened as she reached the second floor and she recognised her cook.

'Good afternoon, Bulfinch[2],' said Mrs Albert Forrester with dignity[2]. 'I wish to see my husband.'

'Come in, ma'am,' said Mrs Bulfinch. She turned her head. 'Albert, here's Mrs Forrester come to see you.'

Mrs Forrester stepped into the room and found Albert sitting in a shabby armchair by the fire. He did not have his jacket on and he was wearing his slippers. He was sitting in the armchair reading a newspaper and smoking a cigar. Mrs Bulfinch followed her visitor into the room and closed the door.

'How are you, my dear?' said Albert cheerfully. 'I hope you are well.'

'Won't you sit down, Mrs Forrester,' said Mrs Bulfinch, dusting a chair and pushing it forward.

Mrs Albert Forrester nodded at Mrs Bulfinch and sat down.

'I would have preferred to see you alone, Albert,' she said. There was laughter in his eyes.

'Anything you have to say is Mrs Bulfinch's business as well as mine. I think it is better that she is here with us.'

'As you wish,' Mrs Albert Forrester replied quietly.

Mrs Bulfinch pulled up a chair and sat down. Mrs Albert Forrester saw her clearly for the first time. She was a woman of about forty-five, with reddish hair and a reddish face. She was not pretty, but she looked a kind person.

Mrs Forrester stepped into the room and found Albert sitting in a shabby armchair by the fire.

'Well, my dear, what do you want to say to me?' asked Albert.

Mrs Albert Forrester smiled at him. She tried to look as friendly as she could.

'You must know that this is ridiculous, Albert,' she said. 'I have come to take you home.'

'Nothing you say will persuade[5] me to live with you again,' replied Albert. The words sounded hard, but his voice was friendly.

'You're not serious.'

'Yes, I am.'

'Do you love this woman?'

'We get on well together, don't we old girl[2]?' said Albert, looking at Mrs Bulfinch with a loving smile.

Mrs Albert Forrester noticed the loving words: 'old girl'. He had never used affectionate words like those to her.

'Have you not been happy with me, Albert?' she asked.

'We've been married for thirty-five years, my dear,' he replied. 'That's too long – much too long. You're a good woman, but you are a literary person and I am not.'

'But I have always talked to you about my interests. You have come to my lunch-parties and talked to my friends. You cannot say that I left you out of things.'

'Yes, you did not leave me out of things,' said Albert. 'Don't remind me of those dreadful lunch-parties and the dreadful people who came to them! I disliked every one of them!'

Mrs Albert Forrester began to grow desperate[3]. 'But we have been together for thirty-five years. Don't all those years mean anything to you? I'm used to you. I won't know what to do without you.'

'The new cook has very good references,' said Mrs Bulfinch. 'All you have to do is tell her how many are coming for lunch. She will do the rest.'

Mrs Albert Forrester did not know how to reply to this remark.

'You are wasting your time here,' went on Albert. 'I have made my decision and I am going to keep to it. I shall, of course, give you as much money as I can.'

'Albert has worked long enough,' Mrs Bulfinch said. 'It's time he retired and started enjoying life. I've got a small house in a seaside town and we are going to live there.'

'I've discussed this matter at work,' said Albert. 'I have sold my share of the business. When everything is arranged, I shall have an income of nine hundred pounds a year – that's three hundred pounds for each of us.'

'But how can I live on three hundred pounds a year?' asked Mrs Forrester in dismay.

'You have a literary reputation,' replied Albert. 'You must write more books and make money from your writing.'

'You know very well that I don't get any money from my books. My books bring me a reputation, but they don't bring me any money.'

It was then that Mrs Bulfinch had an idea. She had an idea which was going to change Mrs Albert Forrester's life.

'Why don't you write a good, thrilling detective story?' she asked.

'Me?' exclaimed Mrs Albert Forrester. 'With my reputation? I have a reputation for writing works of literature – not detective stories.'

'It's not a bad idea,' said Albert. 'It's not a bad idea at all. And I'm sure it would not harm your reputation. The critics must find your books as difficult to read as I do. Give them a book they enjoy reading and they will thank you.'

'The idea is mad,' insisted Mrs Albert Forrester. 'I could never please the public.'

'Why not?' asked Albert. 'The public want to read good writing, but they don't want to be bored. Everyone knows your name, but who wants to read your books? No one wants to read them because they're boring.'

'My books are of the highest literary merit,' insisted Mrs Albert Forrester.

'If you write a thrilling detective story in good English,' replied Albert, 'ordinary people – the general public – will enjoy it, the critics will enjoy it too and praise it highly. You will make a fortune from such a book.'

'Of course, it will have to be a good detective story,' said Mrs Bulfinch. 'You don't want love and romance in a good detective story. What you want is murder. Give me a story which begins with a lady in evening dress, wearing lots of diamonds, lying dead on the carpet with a dagger in her heart.'

'No, no,' interrupted Albert. 'That's not the way to start. I like stories which begin with a very respectable-looking[2], middle-aged, well-dressed gentleman, wearing a gold watch on a chain, lying dead in Hyde Park.

'People like to read about the murder of a respectable-looking, middle-aged, gentleman,' he went on. 'People like to think that everyone has something to hide – even respectable-looking, middle-aged gentlemen.'

'Yes, I see what you mean, Albert,' said Mrs Bulfinch. 'The murdered gentleman was a solicitor[5] who knew some terrible family secret.'

'Exactly,' said Albert to Mrs Forrester. 'We can give you lots of ideas. I've read hundreds of detective stories. That's what brought me and Mrs Bulfinch together. I gave her every story to read after I had read it.'

Mrs Albert Forrester stood up with great dignity.

'I see it is hopeless,' she said. 'I came here to persuade you to come back with me. But now I see how different we are. You have lived in a house surrounded by the best of English literature and you have spent your time reading detective stories.'

'Hundreds and hundreds!' said Albert proudly.

'I will go now,' said Mrs Albert Forrester. 'There is nothing more to say.'

'Very well, my dear,' said Albert. 'But think about our idea of writing a really good detective story.'

Mrs Bulfinch showed Mrs Forrester down the stairs.

'Don't you worry about Albert,' said Mrs Bulfinch. 'I'll take care of him. Now that he's retired, he must have a new interest to keep him busy. He's going to take up stamp-collecting.'

Mrs Albert Forrester heard these words with great surprise. Albert collecting postage stamps! What a strange idea! But just then a tram came along and Mrs Albert Forrester hurried to catch it.

She sat down in the tram and felt dismayed. What was she going to say to Mr Simmons? He would be waiting at the flat when she got back. And so would the others. What would she say to them?

She wondered what the time was and looked up at the man sitting opposite her. She was amazed. The man was a respectable-looking, middle-aged, well-dressed gentleman, wearing a gold watch on a chain.

He looked exactly like the man that Albert had described. He wore a silk hat, a black coat, black trousers and was carrying a briefcase. Mrs Albert Forrester was sure that he was a solicitor.

The gentleman stood up and got off the tram at the next stop. Mrs Albert Forrester watched him go down a narrow, dirty street. She wondered where he was going and why. What business would a well-dressed gentleman have in such a poor street?

She got off the tram at Victoria Station and took a bus to Marble Arch. But she was afraid to go back home and meet Simmons and the others. She got off the bus at Hyde Park and walked slowly along the path in the park.

As she walked, she thought about what Albert and Mrs Bulfinch had said.

Why not? she asked herself. Other famous writers have written detective stories. Why can't I?

When she came to the well-known statue called the Achilles Statue, she stopped for a moment. She had an idea.

After a few minutes, she left the Achilles Statue and walked to her flat. When she opened the door, she found them all waiting for her.

'Here she is,' said Rose Waterford.

Mr Simmons, Clifford Boylestone, Harry Oakland and Oscar Charles were all there. Mrs Albert Forrester shook hands with them all.

'I'm so sorry,' she said. 'I'm terribly late. And you have been kept waiting for your tea. I haven't any idea what the time is.'

'Well?' they said. 'What happened?'

They all wanted to hear what had happened at four hundred and eleven Kennington Road. But Mrs Albert Forrester had a surprise for them.

21

'My dears,' she began, 'I've got the most wonderful news. I've had a marvellous idea.'

She paused for a few moments.

'I'M GOING TO WRITE A DETECTIVE STORY.'

They stared at her with open mouths. She held up her hand to prevent them speaking, although none of them wanted to say anything. They did not know what to say.

'I'm going to write a detective story which will be a great work of literature. It will be a thrilling story and it will be well written. The idea came to me as I was walking in Hyde Park. It's a murder story. It shall begin with the murder of a very respectable-looking, middle-aged, well-dressed gentleman in Hyde Park and I shall call it *The Achilles Statue*.'

'What a wonderful title!' exclaimed Mr Simmons. 'Everyone will want to buy a book with that title and your name on it.'

'But what about Albert?' asked Clifford Boylestone.

'Albert?' repeated Mrs Forrester. 'Albert?'

She looked at Boylestone as if she did not know what he was talking about.

'Oh, Albert! I knew there was something I had to do. But when I was walking in Hyde Park I had this idea and I forgot all about him. What a fool you will think I am.'

'Then you haven't seen Albert?'

'My dear, I forgot all about him. Let Albert keep his cook. I can't worry about Albert now. I am going to write a detective story.'

THE ROUND DOZEN

One November, in the early 1920s, I was very ill with influenza[5]. London is always cold and wet in winter. It is not a good place to stay after an illness. To get my strength back, I decided to go and stay for a few weeks at Elsom, a small seaside town in the South of England.

In the summer, lots of holiday-makers come to Elsom. Then the boarding houses[5] are full and the restaurants and cafés are busy.

It is much quieter in winter, but there are always a few visitors. These are usually elderly people who are looking for peace and quiet and who find the cheaper prices in the winter months very attractive.

Whenever I visited Elsom, I always stayed at the Dolphin, a small hotel on the seafront[5]. I arrived at Elsom in the afternoon. After I had unpacked my case, I went for a walk. Clouds covered the sky and the flat sea was grey and cold.

No one was sitting on the seats on the seafront, but a few people were walking up and down. My heart sank[3]. Life suddenly seemed dull and empty. I walked back to the hotel, went to my room and sat down to read a book.

I was glad when it was time to go down for dinner. I went into the dining-room. The other guests of the hotel were already seated at their tables. There was a middle-aged lady sitting by herself and two elderly gentlemen at another table.

There were three other people sitting together in the dining-room: an old gentleman and two ladies. One of the ladies was old and probably the gentleman's wife. The other lady was younger and possibly his daughter. The older lady made me smile. She was dressed in the fashion of many years ago – a large black dress and a black bonnet.

The younger lady was sitting with her back to me and I could not see her face. But I noticed that she had long, brown hair which was neatly arranged on the back of her head. She wore a grey dress.

After a few moments, she turned her head and I was able to see her face. I was greatly surprised. She was very, very beautiful. Her nose was small and straight and her chin was perfectly shaped. The careful arrangement of her hair added to the beauty of her face.

When dinner was finished, the three of them stood up. The old lady walked straight out of the room, looking neither to the right nor to the left. The beautiful young lady followed her.

Then I got my greatest surprise. The beautiful lady was not young – she was quite old. She was wearing a simple grey dress which was rather old-fashioned[2]. But it was not the kind of dress worn by an older person. It was the kind of dress worn by a girl. She was tall and graceful[5]. She was not a young woman. But when she was a young woman she must have been remarkably beautiful.

The gentleman stood up and followed the ladies. I had a good look at him. He was a small man, not nearly as tall as his wife. He had lots of curling grey hair. There was nothing unusual about him except his clothes, which were extremely old-fashioned.

When I had finished my dinner, I went out into the hall. I wanted to find out who these old-fashioned people were so I had a look in the visitors' book[5]. I saw their names: Mr and Mrs Edwin St Clair and Miss Porchester.

I asked the manageress who Mr St Clair was. She did not know much about him. She believed Mr St Clair worked in the City. I also learnt that Miss Porchester was their niece and not their daughter.

On my way upstairs to my room, I passed through the lounge. The three of them were sitting in a corner of the room. Mrs St Clair was knitting[5], Miss Porchester was busy with embroidery[5], and Mr St Clair was reading aloud in a quiet voice. As I passed by them, I realised that he was reading from Dickens' *Bleak House*.

Mrs St Clair was knitting, Miss Porchester was busy
with embroidery, and Mr St Clair was reading aloud.

The next day, I went for a walk. On my way back to the Dolphin, I sat down for a rest on one of the seats on the seafront. It was not quite so cold as the day before.

I noticed a man coming towards me. As he came nearer, I saw that he was rather a shabby little man. He wore a thin black coat and a shabby bowler hat. He looked cold and walked with his hands in his pockets.

As he walked past me, he gave me a quick look. He went on a few steps, stopped and turned back. When he came to the seat where I was sitting, he took his hands out of his pockets and greeted me by touching his hat.

I noticed that he was wearing shabby black gloves.

'Excuse me, sir,' he said, 'have you got a match?'

'Certainly.'

He sat down beside me and while I put my hand in my pocket for matches he looked in his pockets for cigarettes. He took out a small paper packet, opened it, and looked dismayed.

'Oh dear! How very annoying! I haven't got a cigarette left.'

'Have one of mine,' I replied, smiling.

I took out my cigarette case and offered him one. Sadly, he looked down at his boots, which were in need of repair. He was a tired-looking man with a long thin nose and pale blue eyes. I was not sure of his age. He could have been any age between thirty-five and sixty.

Although he was poor, he was clean and neat. He was trying hard to look respectable.

'Are you staying here long, sir?' he asked me.

'Ten days or a fortnight.'

'Is this your first visit to Elsom, sir?'

'I have been here before.'

'I know this town well, sir. There are very few seaside towns that I have not visited. Elsom is one of the best, sir. It's a highly respectable place. And I have a very happy memory of Elsom. I was married here in St Martin's Church.

'Really?' I said.

'It was a very happy marriage, sir.'

'I'm glad to hear it,' I replied.

'Nine months, that one lasted,' he said thoughtfully.

I immediately thought that this was a very strange remark. I had not wanted to listen to the sad story of his married life. But this strange remark – 'Nine months, that one lasted' – made me curious[3]. I waited to hear more. But I was disappointed. He sighed[3] and sat staring in front of him without speaking. At last, I broke the silence.

'There aren't many people here,' I said.

'I like it like this. I'm not a person who likes crowds. As I said a moment ago, I've been to almost every seaside town in England. But I never go anywhere in the summer. It's the winter I like.'

'Don't you find it melancholy[3]?'

He turned towards me and put his black-gloved hand on my arm.

'It is melancholy. And that's what I like about it. Because it's melancholy, people find a little ray of sunshine very welcome.'

I could not understand this remark. It did not seem to make any sense at all so I did not reply. He took his hand away and got up.

'But I musn't keep you, sir. Pleased to have met you.'

He took off his shabby hat and bowed[5] to me very politely. Then he walked slowly away. It was beginning to get cold so I got up and walked back to the Dolphin.

Later that day, I talked to the manageress and learnt a little more about Mr St Clair, his wife and niece. They stayed by themselves and did not mix with the other guests. I became quite interested in these three strange people who wore such old-fashioned clothes.

When I met them on the stairs, I bowed and received a polite bow in return. But they did not smile and they did not speak. Then one afternoon, when I was sitting in my room, the porter came to

27

see me. Mr St Clair had sent him to ask me for a book. I told the porter to tell Mr St Clair that I was sorry. I did not have the book he wanted.

What a strange way of making a request, I thought. Why had Mr St Clair sent the porter? Why had he not come himself? They were most unusual people.

But this strange request gave me the chance I was looking for. That evening after dinner, I went into the lounge and spoke to Mr St Clair.

'I'm sorry I haven't got the book you wanted,' I said.

Mr St Clair was surprised that I had spoken to him.

'It does not matter,' he said.

But I was able then to start a conversation. We talked about writers and about books. Mr St Clair and his wife believed that things had changed for the worse since they were young. Since those days, people's behaviour had got worse and modern writers wrote improper[2] books.

This explained why they dressed in such old-fashioned clothes. Their clothes showed how they felt. They believed that people did not behave properly any more. Their clothes were old-fashioned; and so were their beliefs and attitudes[2].

During the conversation, Miss Porchester said that she had read some books by modern writers. Her aunt and uncle were surprised to hear that.

'But you said I could read any book I liked after I was thirty,' she said.

'Any book you like, my dear,' said Mrs St Clair, 'but not an improper book.'

'There is a difference, my dear Eleanor,' said Mr St Clair, 'between you reading any book you like and you reading a book that we do not approve of.'

I could not see this difference. But I said nothing. Did their niece, Miss Porchester, believe the same things as they did? As they talked, I began to wonder about this.

Next morning, as I was walking through a pretty lane in Elsom, I met Miss Porchester who was taking a walk. She bowed as I passed her and she blushed[3]. A few yards behind her I saw the funny, shabby little man with gloves. He touched his bowler hat.

'Excuse me, sir, could you let me have a match, please?' he said.

'Certainly,' I replied, 'but I'm afraid I have no cigarettes with me.'

'May I offer you one of mine?' he said, taking out the paper packet. It was empty, as usual.

'Oh dear, I haven't got one either. How odd.'

He walked on and seemed to be hurrying. I began to have doubts about him. Was he following Miss Porchester? For a moment, I thought of going after him, but I did not. He was a very polite little man. I was sure he would not try to annoy Miss Porchester.

I saw him again that afternoon. I was sitting on the seafront. He walked towards me with little, short steps. He looked like a dried leaf being pushed along by the wind. This time he sat down beside me straightaway.

I did not wait for him to ask me for a match, but at once offered him a cigarette.

'How very kind of you, sir!'

He lit the cigarette and sat smoking and looking out at the sea. Then he turned to me once more.

'Excuse me, sir,' he said, 'but am I right in thinking that you are the well-known author?'

'I am an author,' I replied. 'But how did you know me?'

'I've seen your photograph in the newspapers,' he said. 'I suppose you don't know *me*?'

I looked at him again, a shabby little man in neat but shabby black clothes, with a long nose and pale blue eyes.

'I'm afraid I don't,' I said.

'I suppose I have changed a lot,' he sighed. 'There was a time when my photograph was on the front page of every newspaper.'

He was silent for a while as he looked out over the cold, grey winter sea. Then he turned again towards me.

'It must be very interesting to be an author, sir,' he said. 'I have often thought that I would try writing myself. I believe I could write a book if I tried.

'There are not many people who have lived the life I have lived,' he went on. 'I did write to one of the Sunday newspapers about it once, but they never answered my letter.

'Of course, you don't know who I am, sir, do you?' he continued.

'I'm afraid I don't.'

He sat for a moment, thinking of himself. He was trying to come to a decision. Then he turned to me and said with pride: 'I am the famous Mortimer Ellis.'

'Oh?'

I did not know what to say other than my very weak 'Oh?'. I was sure that I had never heard that name in my life before. I saw that he was deeply disappointed.

'Mortimer Ellis,' he repeated. 'You've never heard of me?'

I had to confess that I had never heard of him.

'Fame never lasts,' he said bitterly. 'For weeks I was the most famous man in England. Look at me. You must have seen my photograph in the newspapers. Mortimer Ellis.'

'I'm sorry,' I said, shaking my head.

He paused for a moment to make what he had to say sound more important.

'I'm the well-known bigamist[4]. I've had eleven wives, sir.'

I did not know what to say. What do you say to someone who has just told you that he has been married to eleven women at the same time? I was speechless.

'Yes, I've had eleven wives, sir,' he repeated.

Finally, I managed to ask him the only question I could think of.

'But why did you stop at eleven?'

'I knew you would ask me that question,' he said quickly. 'The moment I saw you I knew that you were intelligent. Three, they say, is a lucky number. And so is nine. Ten is all right. But eleven! There's something wrong with eleven. It doesn't sound complete. That's my one regret in life. I should have liked to have made it twelve. That's the number I would have liked to have made it: the Round Dozen.'

I had to agree with him. There is something incomplete about eleven. In England, we never buy eleven eggs or nine eggs or even ten eggs: we buy eggs by the dozen: a round dozen.

The shabby little man searched in his inside pocket and brought out a thick, very greasy, pocket-book. From this, he took a large bundle of newspaper cuttings[5]. They were creased and dirty.

The cuttings were long. Many of them were from the front pages of the newspapers. He had been famous in his time. One was headed, "A Much Married Man"; another, "Heartless Scoundrel Punished".

I quickly looked through the report I was holding.

'I see you were sent to prison for five years.'

'Disgraceful, it was. It was the judge – he was to blame. But it didn't do him much good. He died a year later.'

'May I read them?' I asked him.

'Of course,' he replied. 'That's why I gave them to you. I want you to read them. And see what you think after you've read them. I'm sure that you'll agree that I was badly treated.'

As I read the newspaper cuttings, I understood why he knew the seaside towns of England so well. They were his hunting-grounds. He used to go to a seaside town in the winter when it was quiet. He would take a room in one of the empty boarding houses. He would then make friends with a woman who was a widow or a spinster[4] and who was beginning to grow old. I noticed that all their ages were between thirty-five and fifty.

I quickly looked through the report I was holding.

They had all said in court that they had met him first on the seafront. Within a fortnight of their meeting he had proposed marriage to them and they were married shortly after. Soon after their marriage, he would persuade them to give him any savings they had. Once he had their money, he left them, never to return.

They were all respectable women; one was the daughter of a doctor and another the daughter of a clergyman[5]. Their savings were usually between five hundred and a thousand pounds. And he had robbed them all.

The strange thing was that they all agreed that he had been an excellent husband. Not only did they ask for mercy to be shown to him, but one said that she was willing to have him back again. Quite remarkable!

I looked closely at the shabby little man who was sitting on the bench beside me.

'I hope you won't mind me asking,' I said, 'and I hope you don't think my question rude, but . . . why did they marry you?'

'Because I asked them,' he replied, surprised by my question.

I sat and thought about his strange life. Then I noticed that he was smiling.

'Now I understand what you mean by your question,' he said. 'You think that I am not handsome and women want to marry handsome men. No, no, sir, you're quite wrong. Women may like men with good looks, but they don't want to marry them.

'They think that good-looking men are not serious. What they want is a man who is serious. And the next thing they want is attention. I may not be handsome, but believe me, sir, I've got what every woman wants. And the proof is, I made all of my wives happy.

'Attention, sir, that's what women want. I never went out of the house without giving my wife a kiss. And I never came in without giving her another. And I never forgot to bring her a present – a box of chocolates or a bunch of flowers. I never worried about the expense.'

'Why should you?' I asked. 'It was her money you were spending.'

'And what's wrong with that? It's not the money you've spent on a present that's important, it's the fact that you've remembered to get one. That's what is important with women.'

I looked again at the newspaper cuttings which I was still holding.

'I'll tell you what surprises me,' I said. 'All these women were very respectable, older persons. And yet, after a very short friendship, they married you without finding out anything about you. Isn't that strange?'

'Not at all, sir. The fact is that a respectable middle-aged woman wants to be married. She'll do anything to get married. Eleven times! Why that's nothing. I could have been married thirty times if I'd wanted to.'

I gave him back his newspaper cuttings. He folded them up neatly and put them back in his greasy pocket-book.

'You know, sir, I don't believe I'm a bad man. People shouted and threw things at me when I was taken to prison. But did any of them ever ask themselves what I had done for those women?'

'You took their money.'

'Of course I took their money. I have to have money to live on the same as everybody else. But what did I give them in exchange? I'll tell you what I gave them in exchange. I gave them romance. Look at this place.'

He stretched out his arm and swung it round pointing to the sea, the sky, the boarding houses.

'There are a hundred places like this in England. All dull and melancholy. Doesn't it make your heart sink? And think of all those women who come here. They hardly know anyone. They've just enough money to live on and that's all. They live their lives walking along one long seafront that goes on from one dull seaside town to another.

'Even in the summer there's nothing for them. They might as well be dead. And then I come along – a little ray of sunshine. I give them love and attention. I give them romance. I bring them change and excitement. You may think I'm a criminal – you're wrong. It's the opposite. Five years in prison, they gave me! They should have given me a medal for all the good I did for those women.'

He took out his empty cigarette packet and shook it sadly.

'Here, have one of mine,' I said.

He took a cigarette without a word.

'And what have I got out of it?' he went on after a short pause. 'Enough money to pay for a room in a cheap boarding house and some cigarettes. That's all. And now my pockets are empty.'

He looked at me sadly.

'I've never asked anyone for money in my life,' he said. 'But I was wondering if you could lend me a little. A pound would do, sir.'

I had enjoyed listening to the bigamist's story. I thought it was worth a pound. I took out my pocket-book and pulled out a bank note.

'I suppose you couldn't make it two pounds, sir?'

I handed him a couple of pounds and he gave a little sigh as he took them.

'There's one thing I'd like you to explain to me,' I said as I put my pocket-book away. 'All those women gave you their savings. How did you persuade them to do that?'

'I promised them more, sir. Tell a woman that you know how to double their money, and she'll rush to hand it over to you. Greed, sir. Plain greed.'

———

One evening a few days later, I was having a drink with Mr St Clair and he told me the story of Miss Porchester. She had been engaged to be married to a nephew of Mr St Clair, a solicitor.

Then there was a scandal. They discovered that he was having an affair with the daughter of his laundress – the woman who washed his clothes.

'It was a terrible business,' said Mr St Clair. 'Terrible. But of course my niece did the right thing. She sent her cousin back the engagement ring, his letters and his photograph. It broke her heart[3].'

'Miss Porchester is a remarkably handsome woman,' I said. 'When she was younger, she must have been very beautiful. Why didn't she marry someone else?'

'Yes, Miss Porchester was very beautiful. But she never loved anyone else except her cousin. She never speaks of him and it is now more than thirty years since she last saw him. But I am certain that she still loves him. She will never love another man.'

But Mr St Clair was wrong – quite wrong. You can never tell what a woman will do next. Mr St Clair had known Miss Porchester for many years. When her parents had died, Mr and Mrs St Clair had brought her up as their own child. But what did they really know about her? Very little, I'm afraid – as the rest of this story will make clear.

––––

Two days after Mr St Clair had told me the sad story of Miss Porchester's life – a story that explained why Miss Porchester had never married – something terrible happened.

It was the afternoon and I had been out for a walk. When I returned to the Dolphin, I was met by the manageress who was very excited.

'Mr St Clair would like to see you immediately,' she said. 'Would you go up to their room, number twenty-seven.'

'Certainly. But why?'

'Oh, something terrible has happened. They'll tell you all about it.'

I knocked at the door. I heard a voice telling me to come in.

36

I entered the room. Mrs St Clair was lying on the sofa with a handkerchief soaked in eau-de-cologne on her forehead. She was crying. Mr St Clair was standing in front of the fire.

'I'm sorry to have to ask you to come here,' he began. 'But we are in great distress[3] and we thought you might be able to help us.' He was very upset.

'What *has* happened?'

'Our niece, Miss Porchester, has eloped.'

Mrs St Clair gave a loud cry. Mr St Clair went on with his story.

'This morning she told us she had a headache. She asked to be left alone in her room. This afternoon my wife went to see if there was anything she could do for her. The room was empty. All her clothes had gone and so had all her jewellery. There was a letter on the bed telling us what she had done.'

'I'm sorry,' I said. 'But I don't see how I can help you.'

'We thought that you were the only gentleman in Elsom that she knew.'

Then I understood his meaning.

'It's not me,' I said. 'I haven't eloped with her.'

'Yes, I can see you haven't eloped with her. At first we thought perhaps . . . but, if it isn't you, who is it?'.

'I'm sure I don't know.'

'I will never forgive her,' said Mr St Clair.

'But is there any reason why Miss Porchester should not get married?' I asked.

'At her age?' he answered angrily. 'It's ridiculous. Everyone will laugh at us. Do you know how old she is? She's fifty-one.'

'Fifty-four,' said Mrs St Clair.

'And who is this man she has married?' went on Mr St Clair. 'She must have been meeting him here in Elsom without us knowing anything about it. We don't even know his name. I fear that something terrible has happened to her.'

Suddenly I had an idea. That morning after breakfast, I had

Mrs St Clair was lying on the sofa with a handkerchief soaked in eau-de-cologne on her forehead.

gone out to buy cigarettes and I had met Mortimer Ellis. I had not seen him for several days.

His boots had been repaired and were shining brightly. His hat was brushed, he was wearing a shirt with a clean collar, and he had new gloves. I thought, at the time, that he had spent my two pounds very wisely.

Then I remembered something else. I remembered the time I had seen him walking behind Miss Porchester. Was it possible that they had been walking together and that he had stopped when they saw me? Suddenly I understood it all.

'Did Miss Porchester have some money of her own?' I asked.

'A little. She has three thousand pounds.'

Suddenly Mrs St Clair sprang to her feet with a cry.

'Edwin, Edwin, what if he takes her away and doesn't marry her?'

'That would be a terrible scandal. It would kill me,' he cried.

'Don't be afraid,' I said. 'He'll marry her all right. He always does. He'll marry her in church.'

They must have thought I was mad. But I was certain now that I knew what had happened. Mortimer Ellis had succeeded. He had married Miss Porchester and made the *Round Dozen*.

*That morning, I met Mortimer Ellis. . . . I thought that
he had spent my two pounds wisely.*

JANE

I remember very clearly the first time I saw Jane Fowler. I had been travelling in China and shortly after my return to London, I was invited to tea with an old friend, Mrs Tower.

Since my last visit, everything in Mrs Tower's lounge had been changed.

'Do you remember this room as it used to be?' she asked. 'The lights were so bright and glaring. Now they are quiet and subdued[5].'

'I prefer brighter lights which help me to see clearly,' I said.

'But sometimes I don't want people to see me too clearly,' laughed Mrs Tower. 'In this subdued lighting, people will say what a young face I have.'

I had no idea how old she was. She told everyone that she was forty. But she had been forty for some years now. She did not try to hide the fact that she dyed her hair. It was a pretty reddish-brown colour. she also used make-up, but she used it well. She was a handsome woman, very well-dressed, and in the subdued glow of the new lighting, she did not look a day more than forty.

We talked pleasantly and Mrs Tower gave me all the news about our friends. It was very pleasant to sit in a comfortable chair in front of a brightly burning fire and drink tea. As I was getting ready to leave, we arranged to meet again. We decided on a date for me to come and have dinner with Mrs Tower. Then she added a puzzling[3] remark.

'But I must warn you. If Jane Fowler is here, I shall have to cancel the invitation.'

'Who is Jane Fowler?' I asked.

'Jane Fowler is my sister-in-law. She was my husband's sister and she married a manufacturer[5] in the North. She's been a widow for many years and she's very wealthy. Jane Fowler worries me a lot.'

'Why does she worry you a lot?' I asked.

'She doesn't know how to live in London society,' replied Mrs Tower. 'She doesn't know how to dress fashionably or how to put on make-up. She looks twenty years older than I do. But she loves to tell people that we were at school together.

'I am her only living relative, and she is very fond of me. When she comes to London, she always stays here with me. She would never think of staying anywhere else.

'We sit here and she knits and reads. Sometimes, she takes me out to a fashionable restaurant. But she dresses like a charwoman[2]. And when we do go out, there is always someone who knows me sitting at the next table.'

Mrs Tower stopped to take a breath.

'I'm sure you know how to deal with a woman like that,' I said.

'You don't understand,' she said. 'I can't upset her. She is so kind. And she has a heart of gold[3]. She bores me to death, but I wouldn't do anything to upset her.'

'And when does she arrive?' I asked.

'Tomorrow.'

But Mrs Tower had no sooner given this reply than the door-bell rang. There were sounds in the hall and in a few moments the butler[2] showed an elderly lady into the room.

'Mrs Fowler,' he announced.

'Jane,' cried Mrs Tower, 'I was not expecting you to arrive today.'

'So your butler has just told me. But I certainly said today in my letter.'

'Well, it doesn't matter. I'm very glad to see you whenever you come. Fortunately, I have no plans for this evening.'

I had a quiet laugh to myself. I knew that Mrs Tower and

Jane Fowler were the same age. And Mrs Fowler looked at least fifty-five. So Mrs Tower was certainly much older than forty.

Jane Fowler was a big woman. She wore a black hat with a wide brim and from the brim a thin black veil hung down over her shoulders. Her long black dress was covered by a cloak which reached down to a pair of strong boots. she was short-sighted and she wore large, gold-rimmed spectacles.

Mrs Fowler took off her cloak and her hat and placed them all together on the sofa in the corner. I wondered where Mrs Fowler had her clothes made. They were expensive clothes, but they were very old-fashioned.

Mrs Fowler's grey hair was combed straight back and her large forehead and ears showed clearly. But when she smiled she showed small, white teeth. They were beautiful. Her smile was certainly very sweet.

The next morning, Mrs Tower rang me up. She sounded very cheerful.

'I've got the most wonderful news for you,' she said. 'Jane is going to be married.'

I could not believe my ears[5].

'Her fiancé is coming here to dinner tonight. I am sure you would like to meet the man Jane is going to marry. Please do come.'

'Who is he?' I asked.

'I don't know. She says that he is an architect[5].'

I agreed to accept the invitation.

When I arrived, Mrs Tower was alone. She looked very handsome in a bright gown, which was a little too young for her.

'Jane is getting dressed,' she told me. 'She's very excited. She says she adores him. His name is Gilbert and when she speaks about him her voice goes very soft. It makes me want to laugh.'

'I wonder what he's like.'

'Oh, I'm sure I can guess,' she replied. 'He will be a very large, fat man with a bald head. And he will have a red face and a loud voice.'

Mrs Fowler came in. She wore a black silk dress with a wide skirt. She had on a diamond and silver necklace.

Mrs Tower praised her.

'You're looking very pretty tonight, my dear.' In fact, she did look pretty and when she greeted me she gave me a sweet smile.

'Congratulations on your engagement,' I said.

'Don't do that until you've seen my young man.'

'It's very sweet of you to refer to your fiancé as a young man,' said Mrs Tower.

Mrs Fowler's eyes shone behind her large, gold spectacles.

'Now don't expect anyone too old,' she said. 'You wouldn't want me to marry an old man with one foot in the grave[5] would you?'

This was the only warning she gave us. There was no time for further discussion of her fiancé's age for the butler flung open the door and announced in a loud voice: 'Mr Gilbert Napier.'

A well-dressed young man entered the room. He was not very tall. He had fair hair and blue eyes. He was certainly not more than twenty-four years old. I immediately thought that Mrs Fowler's fiancé was a widower and that this was his son. He had sent his son to tell Mrs Fowler that he was ill and could not come to dinner.

But I was completely wrong. The moment he saw Mrs Fowler, the young man smiled brightly and he went towards her with both hands outstretched. Mrs Fowler took his hands and, with a quiet smile on her lips, turned to her sister-in-law.

'Marion,' she said. 'This is my young man.'

He held out his hand to Mrs Tower.

I watched Mrs Tower's face. It was wonderful how she behaved. She wanted to show the astonishment and dismay she felt. But she was able to control herself. Her astonishment and dismay showed themselves in her face for a moment. But

*Her astonishment and dismay showed themselves in her face
for a moment.*

then they disappeared immediately. She even managed to give the young man a smile. But she was unable to say a word. Mrs Fowler kept perfectly calm.

'I know you'll like him, Marion,' she said.

I shall never forget that meal. It was the most amusing meal I have ever been present at. Mrs Tower could not decide what her friend, Mrs Fowler, was doing. Was she playing a joke? Was she trying to make her friend look foolish? But Jane never made jokes and she could never do anything cruel.

Mrs Tower was amazed, puzzled and annoyed. But she talked brightly and cheerily throughout the excellent dinner.

I wondered if Gilbert Napier saw the hard looks she was secretly giving him. She was trying to decide what kind of man he was. And I could see that she was very angry – her face was bright red under her make-up.

'You look rather flushed tonight, Marion,' said Jane, looking at her through her large spectacles.

'Perhaps I've put on too much make-up,' replied Mrs Tower coldly.

Mrs Fowler turned to her young man, smiling shyly.

'Marion and I were at school together. You would never guess that looking at us now, would you? But of course I have lived a very quiet life.'

I do not know what she meant by these remarks. Did she not know that she was making Mrs Tower angry and upset? In fact Mrs Tower was so angry that for once she spoke the truth.

'Neither of us will ever be fifty again, Jane,' she said.

'Gilbert says I must tell everyone I'm forty-nine,' Jane replied calmly.

Mrs Tower's hands shook slightly with anger. But she was able to control herself.

'There is of course a difference between your ages,' she said, with a smile.

'Yes, there's a twenty-seven year difference between our ages,'

Jane replied, 'Do you think it is too much? Gilbert says that I'm very young for my age. I told you I shouldn't want to marry a man with one foot in the grave.'

I really had to laugh and Gilbert laughed too. His laughter was bright and youthful. It seemed that he was amused by everything that Jane said. But I saw that Mrs Tower was not able to control her anger much longer. I felt I had to say something to help her.

'You will be very busy buying your wedding clothes,' I said.

'No,' replied Jane. 'Gilbert is taking care of that. I wanted to get my clothes from the dressmaker in Liverpool who has always made my clothes. But Gilbert would not let me. And I've agreed to do what he wants.'

Jane looked at Gilbert with a loving smile, as though she were a young girl of seventeen. Mrs Tower's face now went quite pale.

'We're going to Italy for our honeymoon,' went on Jane. 'And we shall stop in Paris and I'll buy my new clothes there.'

'Do you expect to be away long?' I asked politely.

'Six months. It will be a wonderful holiday for Gilbert. You see he has never had more than a fortnight's holiday before.'

'Why not?' asked Mrs Tower sharply.

'He's never been able to afford it, poor dear.'

'Ah!' said Mrs Tower. And she put lots of meaning into that one exclamation.

After we had coffee, Mrs Tower said that she had a headache. I suggested to Gilbert that it was time to say goodbye to the ladies and leave.

As soon as we were out of the house, Mrs Tower started questioning her friend.

'Are you crazy, Jane?' she asked.

'No more than most people,' Jane answered calmly.

'Why are you marrying this young man?' asked Mrs Tower, trying to be as polite as possible.

'Because he has asked me five times and he won't take no for an answer. I grew tired of refusing him.'

'And why do you think he wants to marry you?'

'I amuse him.'

Mrs Tower gave an exclamation of annoyance.

'Ha! He's after your money,' she said. 'He's a rascal and I very nearly told him so.'

'You would have been wrong. And it would not have been very polite.'

'He's poor and you're rich. You can't be such a fool. You must see that he's marrying you for your money.'

Jane remained absolutely calm.

'I don't think he is, you know,' she replied. 'I think he's very fond of me.'

'You're an old woman, Jane.'

'I'm the same age as you are, Marion,' she replied.

Mrs Tower's anger was beginning to go out of control.

'I have never let my age show. I'm very young for my age. No one would think that I was more than forty. But even I wouldn't think of marrying a boy twenty-seven years younger than me. Do you believe that it is possible for a young man to love a woman who is old enough to be his mother?'

'I have lived quietly in the country. Perhaps there are things that I don't know . . .'

But Mrs Tower interrupted her without any politeness at all.

'Don't be ridiculous, Jane. I always thought you were a sensible woman. I would never have believed that you would fall in love with a boy.'

'But I am not in love with him. Of course, I'm very fond of him. But I'm not in love with him. I've told him that many times.'

Mrs Tower felt she was going to burst with anger.

'But if you're not in love with him, why are you marrying him?'

'I've been a widow for a long time. I thought I'd like a change.'

'If you are getting married just because you want a change, why don't you marry a man of your own age?'

'No man of my own age has asked me five times to marry him. In fact, no man of my own age has asked me at all.' Jane laughed as she spoke.

'Don't laugh Jane. I won't have it. I think you have gone mad. It's terrible.'

Mrs Tower burst into tears. Jane remained perfectly calm.

'You're going to be so terribly unhappy,' Mrs Tower sobbed and pressed her handkerchief to her eyes. But, as she did so, she took care that she did not spoil her make-up.

'I don't think I will be unhappy,' said Mrs Fowler. 'Gilbert and I have talked it over very carefully. I think I will be able to make him very happy and comfortable. He's never had anyone to look after him properly. And we have decided that if either of us wants a divorce at any time the other will agree.'

Mrs Tower now made a cruel remark.

'How much money has he persuaded you to give him?'

'I wanted to arrange that he should have £1000 a year for life. But he would not accept any money at all. He says he can earn enough for his own needs.'

'Some sort of trick,' was Mrs Tower's sharp reply. 'But now I'm so upset that I must go to bed. We can continue our conversation tomorrow morning.'

'I'm afraid that will not be possible,' replied Mrs Fowler. 'Gilbert and I will be busy arranging the wedding tomorrow morning.'

Mrs Tower raised her hands in dismay. There was nothing more she could say.

———

Mrs Tower and I were at the wedding. Gilbert was smartly dressed and looked very young. He was nervous, but Jane remained calm.

She wore a large dress of silvery-grey and a very large hat with feathers on the top. The hat, together with her gold-rimmed spectacles, made her look quite ridiculous. I was glad when it was over.

We drove with the happy couple to Victoria Station. They were going to Paris on the two o'clock train. As the train left, we waved goodbye. I drove Mrs Tower back to her house.

'How long do you think the marriage will last?' she said. 'Six months?'

'Let's hope it goes well,' I replied, with a smile.

'Don't be foolish. Of course it won't last. She's old and badly-dressed and dull. He'll soon get bored with her. He's marrying her for her money. There's no other reason.'

'Are you sure she's dull?' I said. 'She doesn't say very much, but what she does say is often amusing.'

'I've never heard her make a joke in her life,' was Mrs Tower's sharp reply.

———

Soon after the wedding, I went off again on my travels. I was in the Far East for nearly two years. Mrs Tower did not write many letters and I heard nothing more about the strange marriage of Jane and Gilbert.

But I met Mrs Tower again soon after my return to London. I had been invited to a large dinner-party – there were twenty-four guests. And Mrs Tower was there. I immediately asked about Jane.

'She's very well,' was Mrs Tower's short reply.

'Has the marriage been a success?' I asked.

Mrs Tower paused before replying.

'Yes, it appears to be quite a success.'

'You were wrong then?' I said.

'I said it wouldn't last and I still say it won't last.'

'Is she happy?' I asked.

'They're both happy.'

'Do you see much of them?'

'At first I saw quite a lot of them. But now I don't see them so often. Jane has become very grand and important.'

'What *do* you mean?' I asked with a laugh.

'She's here tonight.'

I looked round the table again. Our hostess[2] was a bright and amusing woman. But I was sure that she would not invite a dull woman like Jane to her dinner-party. Mrs Tower saw that I was puzzled.

'Look at the woman who is sitting to the left of our host,' she said.

I looked. I had noticed the woman who was sitting there when I first came into the room. I had noticed her because she was such a strange-looking woman. I was sure that I had never seen her before.

She was not a young woman, for her hair was grey. She did not try to look younger than she was. She used no lipstick or make-up. Her hair was extremely short and arranged in many curls. Her dress was extraordinary. It was very brightly coloured and looked like a dress that someone would wear to a fancy-dress party[2]. Instead of spectacles, the woman wore a single eyeglass which made her look even odder.

'Is that really your sister-in-law?' I asked in amazement.

'That is Jane Napier,' said Mrs Tower coldly.

At that moment, Mrs Napier was speaking to the host. When she finished speaking, the host burst out laughing and so did the other guests nearby.

A man whom I knew was a famous politician, spoke to Mrs Tower from across the table.

'Your sister-in-law has made another joke, Mrs Tower,' he said.

Mrs Tower smiled coldly.

I had noticed her because she was such a strange-looking woman.

'She's very amusing, isn't she?' added the man.

'What *has* happened to Jane?' I asked Mrs Tower.

Mrs Tower told me the story. While they were in Paris, Gilbert had persuaded Jane to buy new clothes – clothes which were completely different from those she had worn before. Gilbert had designed[5] her dresses himself. He had even persuaded her to throw away the gold-rimmed spectacles and wear an eyeglass.

When they got to Rome, Jane had been embarrassed at first. Whenever she appeared in a hotel lounge, people stopped to stare at her. Then she had got used to it. And, in fact, had begun to enjoy it. Ladies came up to her and asked her where she had bought her dress.

'Do you like it?' Jane answered. 'My husband designed it for me.'

Many of them asked her if she would give them the design so that they could copy it. But Jane always refused. Then she noticed they were watching her closely and trying to remember the design. She spoke to Gilbert about this.

'I don't want other people wearing the same dresses as me,' she said. 'How can I stop them?'

'The only way to do that is to design things that only you can wear.'

'Can you do that?'

'Yes, if you'll do something for me.'

'What's that?'

'Cut your hair very short.'

Jane was not at all happy about this. She was very proud of her long hair. But at last she agreed.

'And that made all the difference,' said Mrs Tower, as she finished the long story. 'When her hair was cut short, she looked unique[5].'

'I can see that that has made a lot of difference,' I replied. 'But changing her clothes and her hair does not explain why she is here tonight in such important company. She has a politician on one side of her and an Admiral-of-the-Fleet[5] on the other.'

'They think Jane is amusing,' said Mrs Tower. 'Didn't you hear them all laughing at what she said?'

I heard the sharpness in Mrs Tower's voice. There was no doubt that there was bitterness in her heart[3]. Mrs Tower used to look down on her sister-in-law. She had always thought of her sister-in-law as a badly-dressed old woman who did not know how to behave in London society. But now this same sister-in-law was the honoured guest at dinner-parties all over London. People came to the dinner-parties just to meet Jane Napier. She had become famous.

'I have been invited here tonight,' added Mrs Tower, 'not because I've known my hostess for twenty years. I have been invited here tonight because I'm Jane Napier's friend!'

That was why Mrs Tower felt so bitter.

After dinner, my hostess came up to me and said: 'I must introduce you to our honoured guest. Do you know Jane Napier? She is the most amusing person in London.'

I was taken to a sofa where Jane was sitting with the Admiral-of-the-Fleet. He showed no sign of moving and Jane introduced him to me.

'Do you know Sir Reginald Frobisher?'

We began to talk. She was the same person that I had known before. But her amazing appearance made everything she said sound unusual. Suddenly I found myself laughing. She had made an amusing remark. It wasn't terribly funny, but the way she said it and the way she looked at me through her eyeglass made it sound extremely amusing. I had to laugh.

She invited me to come and visit her.

'Do come and see us on Tuesday evening. Gilbert will be so glad to see you.'

I went to Jane's on Tuesday evening. I was surprised at the company. The room was full of artists and writers and famous politicians. Jane seemed to be enjoying herself. And her guests were enjoying themselves too. The party did not end until after two o'clock in the morning.

Jane was very popular and she only had to open her mouth and people laughed. But she did seem to me to plan what she was saying. She spoke from her heart[3].

After that, I saw a great deal of Jane Napier. I was often invited to her house. And, also, whenever I was invited out to lunch or dinner, Jane was sure to be there. People no longer wondered why Gilbert had married a woman so much older than himself. They thought he was a very lucky fellow to have such an amusing wife.

Admiral-of-the-Fleet Sir Reginald Frobisher, seemed to be always at the same parties she went to. And he was full of praise for her amusing conversation.

'She's wonderful,' he told everyone. 'She's quite wonderful.'

I became friends with Gilbert. And as I came to know him better, I grew to like him. He was delighted with Jane's success. He was not only proud of her, but truly in love with her.

I once congratulated him on his success.

'Oh, I'm nothing,' he said.

'Nonsense!' I said. 'You made her what she is now. You persuaded her to change her clothes and her hair. But, tell me, how did you make her amusing and popular?'

'But she always was amusing,' he answered.

'You were the only person who thought so,' I replied.

Even Mrs Tower agreed that she had been wrong about Gilbert. She grew fond of him. But she was still sure that the marriage would not last.

'Gilbert is twenty-seven now,' she said to me. 'It's time for a pretty young girl to come along. Did you notice the other evening that pretty young niece of Sir Reginald Frobisher? I thought Jane was looking at her and Gilbert very closely.'

'You once said that the marriage wouldn't last for six months,' I said.

'Now I give it three years,' she replied.

In the end, Mrs Tower was right. But the way it ended did not please her at all. I think she would have preferred to have been wrong.

One day she sent me a message. She wanted me to come straightaway.

'Jane and Gilbert have parted,' she told me at once.

'So, you were right after all,' I said. 'Poor Jane.'

'Poor Jane!' she repeated, in an angry voice. 'It's not at all poor *Jane*. It's poor Gilbert.'

She then told me what had happened. Gilbert had come to her in some distress and told her that Jane had left him.

Mrs Tower had not understood what he was saying.

'I knew it would happen,' she said. 'You were sure to meet a pretty young girl some time. Tell me, who is it?'

'No, no, you don't understand,' he said. 'You don't think I could marry anyone else after being Jane's husband, do you? it's not me who has left Jane. It's Jane who has left me. She wants a divorce and she is going to marry Sir Reginald Frobisher.'

Mrs Tower could not believe her ears.

'But *she* can't divorce *you*,' she said at last.

'But we agreed in the beginning that if either of us wanted a divorce the other would not object.'

'Nonsense,' said Mrs Tower angrily. 'That was because of your age. She knew that you were much younger than her. She knew that at some time you might want to marry someone your own age.'

Mrs Tower tried to argue with Gilbert. She tried to persuade him to change his mind and refuse to get divorced.

'Jane must do as she wants,' he said.

When Gilbert left, Mrs Tower was amazed, puzzled and annoyed. My arrival helped to calm her down a little. But not for long. The door opened and the butler announced the arrival of Jane.

She was dressed in an extraordinary way. I had never seen such a strange hat before. As usual, she was quite calm.

'Gilbert has been here,' Mrs Tower told her.

'Yes, I know. I told him to come and see you. Poor boy. He's quite upset. I'm going to Paris tonight and I want you to be kind to him while I'm away. I'm afraid he'll be rather lonely at first. I'll feel happier if I know that you are taking care of him.'

'He has just told me an amazing story,' Mrs Tower said. 'He tells me you are going to divorce him and marry Sir Reginald Frobisher.'

'Don't you remember that you once advised me to marry a man of my own age?' Jane said quietly. 'The admiral is fifty-three.'

'But Jane, Gilbert made you what you are now,' said Mrs Tower angrily. 'What will you do without him? Without him to design your dresses you'll be nothing.'

'But he's promised to go on designing my dresses,' she said calmly.

'Oh – how *can* you be so cruel and heartless³!'

'But I was never in love with Gilbert,' said Jane. 'I made that clear to him from the beginning. I now feel that I need the friendship of a man of my own age. I think I've been married to Gilbert long enough.'

She paused a little and gave us both a charming smile.

'Of course, I shall make sure that Gilbert is taken care of,' she went on. 'I've arranged that with Reginald. He has a pretty niece that would be right for Gilbert. As soon as we are married, we'll invite them both to stay with us in Malta. That's where we are going to live. The admiral is to be Commander-of-the-Mediterranean-Fleet. And I shouldn't be surprised if the two young people don't fall in love with each other.'

'Have you made the same arrangement with the admiral that you made with Gilbert?' asked Mrs Tower. 'Are both of you free to separate if you want to?'

'The admiral would not agree to that,' Jane replied. 'He says that he has eight large guns on his battleship. And he'll fire them at any man who says he wants to marry me.'

She gave us a strange look through her eyeglass. I knew it would upset Mrs Tower, but I had to laugh.

Mrs Tower gave me an angry look.

'I never thought you were funny, Jane,' she said. 'I cannot understand why people laugh at the things you say.'

'I never thought I was funny, Marion,' said Jane, showing her small bright teeth. 'Perhaps it's a good thing I'm leaving London before other people agree with us.'

'I wish you would tell me the secret of your amazing success,' I said.

'You know, when I married Gilbert and lived in London, people began to laugh at what I said. I could not understand it. At first, I thought it must be my clothes or my hair or my eyeglass. Then I discovered it was because I always spoke the truth.

'Speaking the truth is so unusual that people think it is funny. One of these days, someone else will discover the secret and then everybody will start telling the truth. Then there will be nothing funny about it.'

'But why am I the only person who does not think it funny?' asked Mrs Tower.

'Perhaps that's because you don't know the truth when you hear it, dear,' Jane replied in her usual friendly way.

I felt that Jane had had the last word. I felt that Jane would always have the last word. She was wonderful.

Points for Understanding

1 How old was Mrs Albert Forrester when she wrote *The Achilles Statue*?

2 The critics praised *The Achilles Statue*, but what was more important for Mrs Albert Forrester?

3 The writer of these short stories is Somerset Maugham. What question is Somerset Maugham going to try and answer in this story?

4 Mrs Albert Forrester lived with her husband in a flat not far from Marble Arch.
    (a) Who lived in the best part of the flat?
    (b) Whose tiny bedroom was next to the dark kitchen?
    (c) Who paid the rent of the flat?

5 Somerset Maugham uses words very cleverly. What is he really saying about Mrs Albert Forrester in each of the quotations below?
    (a) Mrs Albert Forrester *did not appear* to be fat. (page 5, line 24) Was she fat or not?
    (b) Her face was large and this made her *look* very intelligent. (page 5, line 25) Was she really very intelligent?
    (c) She *seemed* quite satisfied to be a writer of the highest literary merit. (page 6, lines 19–20) Was she really satisfied?

6 Her Tuesday afternoon tea-parties were famous.
    (a) What kind of people came to Mrs Albert Forrester's tea-parties?
    (b) Why did Mr Albert Forrester never come to these tea-parties?
    (c) What did the guests at the afternoon tea-parties feel they were taking part in?
    (d) When was Mr Albert Forrester always present?

7 It was late in the afternoon when the important event happened.
    (a) What was the important event?
    (b) What was Miss Warren's reaction?

8 Simmons gave two reasons why Mrs Albert Forrester had to get her husband back again.
   (a) What were the two reasons?
   (b) Why did the other guests agree with Simmons?
   (c) What did Mrs Albert Forrester agree to do?
9 'I would have preferred to see you alone,' said Mrs Albert Forrester to her husband. What was his reply?
10 'Do you love this woman?' Mrs Albert Forrester asked her husband. What was his reply?
11 'Albert has worked long enough,' said Mrs Bulfinch.
   (a) What were they planning to do?
   (b) How much money would each of them have?
   (c) Why was Mrs Albert Forrester dismayed by this news?
12 It was then that Mrs Bulfinch had an idea.
   (a) What was Mrs Bulfinch's idea?
   (b) What did Albert think of Mrs Bulfinch's suggestion?
13 How did Albert think that a good detective story should begin?
14 What reason did Mrs Bulfinch suggest for the murder of the respectable-looking, middle-aged, well-dressed gentleman?
15 When Mrs Albert Forrester was on the tram, she looked up at the man sitting opposite her.
   (a) What was the man wearing?
   (b) Why was she sure that he was a solicitor?
   (c) What questions came into her mind when the man got off the tram?
16 Mrs Albert Forrester got off the bus at Hyde Park and walked slowly along the path in the park.
   (a) Where did she stop?
   (b) What idea came into her head?
17 When she opened the door, she found them all waiting for her.
   (a) What did she tell them she was going to do?
   (b) How did Mr Simmons react to her announcement?
   (c) Did she tell the truth when they asked her what happened at Kennington Road?
18 Somerset Maugham began this story by asking how writers got their ideas. What answer do you think he gives to this question?

THE ROUND DOZEN

1 Somerset Maugham decided to go and stay for a few weeks at Elsom.
   (a) Why did he decide to go there?
   (b) What was Elsom like in the summer?
   (c) What is it like in the winter?
2 Which hotel did Somerset Maugham stay in?
3 At dinner, Somerset Maugham saw a group of three people sitting together in the dining-room.
   (a) Why did the older lady make him want to smile?
   (b) Why was he surprised when the younger lady turned her head?
   (c) What surprised him most of all?
4 Somerset Maugham looked in the visitors' book.
   (a) What was the name of the two older people in the group?
   (b) How was Miss Porchester related to them?
5 When Somerset Maugham was sitting on a seat by the seafront, he noticed a man coming towards him.
   (a) How was the man dressed?
   (b) What did the man ask for?
   (c) Do you think the man was really surprised when he discovered that he had no cigarettes?
6 Why did Somerset Maugham think that the man was poor?
7 I immediately thought that this was a very strange remark.
   (a) What was the strange remark?
   (b) Do you think it is a strange remark?
   (c) What other strange remark did the man make?
8 How was Somerset Maugham able to start a conversation with Mr St Clair?
9 Mr St Clair and his wife thought that things had changed for the worse since they were young.
   (a) How had people's behaviour changed?
   (b) What was wrong with modern writers?
   (c) How did the clothes they were wearing show what they felt?
10 There is a difference between you reading any book you like and you reading a book we do not approve of.
   (a) Somerset Maugham could not see any difference. Can you?
   (b) What did Somerset Maugham begin to wonder about?

11 Next morning, Somerset Maugham met Miss Porchester who was taking a walk.
    (a) What did Miss Porchester do as she passed him?
    (b) Who was walking a few yards behind her?
12 What happened when Somerset Maugham told the man that he had no cigarettes?
13 I began to have doubts about him.
    (a) What did Somerset Maugham wonder about the man?
    (b) Why did he decide to do nothing?
14 How did the man know that Somerset Maugham was a well-known author?
15 'I am the famous Mortimer Ellis,' said the man.
    (a) Had Somerset Maugham ever heard of him?
    (b) Why was Mortimer Ellis famous?
16 'But why did you stop at eleven?' Somerset Maugham asked Mortimer Ellis.
    (a) What answer did Mortimer Ellis give to this question?
    (b) How is his answer to the question related to the title of this short story?
17 Why did Mortimer Ellis know the seaside towns of England so well?
18 All of the women that Mortimer Ellis had married were agreed on one thing. What was it?
19 Somerset Maugham asked Mortimer Ellis:
    (a) Why had the women all agreed to marry him?
    (b) Why had they all married him without trying to find out anything about him?
    (c) What answers did he give to these questions?
20 What did Mortimer Ellis say he had given the women in exchange for their money?
21 There are a hundred places like this in England. All dull and melancholy.
    (a) What remark, which Mortimer Ellis made earlier in the story, does this remind you of?
    (b) What was life like for the women who came to these places?
22 How much money did Somerset Maugham give Mortimer Ellis?
23 Somerset Maugham asked him one last question.
    (a) What was the question?
    (b) What reply did Mortimer Ellis give to the question?

24 When she was a young woman, Miss Porchester had been engaged to be married to a nephew of Mrs St Clair. But there had been a scandal.
   (a) What had happened?
   (b) What had Miss Porchester done?
   (c) What was Mr St Clair certain of?
25 How had Mortimer Ellis made the Round Dozen?

JANE

1 'But sometimes I don't want people to see me too clearly,' laughed Mrs Tower.
   (a) Why did Mrs Tower prefer subdued lighting?
   (b) How old did she say she was?
2 'Who is Jane Fowler?' Somerset Maugham asked Mrs Tower. What was her reply?
3 'Jane Fowler worries me a lot,' said Mrs Tower.
   (a) What was wrong with the way Jane Fowler dressed?
   (b) How old did Jane Fowler look?
   (c) What did Jane Fowler love to tell people?
4 Why could Mrs Tower not upset Jane Fowler?
5 Jane Fowler arrived unexpectedly.
   (a) Why did Somerset Maugham have a quiet laugh to himself?
   (b) How did Somerset Maugham know that Jane Fowler was short-sighted?
   (c) Why did Somerset Maugham wonder where Jane Fowler had her clothes made?
   (d) What did Somerset Maugham find pleasing about Jane Fowler?
6 'I've got the most wonderful news for you,' Mrs Tower told Somerset Maugham on the phone.
   (a) What was the wonderful news?
   (b) Why did Mrs Tower want Somerset Maugham to come to dinner that evening?
7 'I wonder what he's like,' Somerset Maugham said to Mrs Tower.
   (a) What was the man's name?
   (b) Why did Mrs Tower want to laugh?
   (c) What did she think the man would be like?

8 'Congratulations on your engagement,' said Somerset Maugham.
  (a) How did Jane Fowler describe her fiancé?
  (b) Why did Mrs Tower think it was sweet of her to describe her fiancé in this way?
  (c) What did Jane Fowler tell them not to expect?
9 The butler flung open the door and announced: 'Mr Gilbert Napier.'
  (a) How old was Mr Gilbert Napier?
  (b) Who did Somerset Maugham think the young man was?
10 I watched Mrs Tower's face. It was wonderful how she behaved. In what way was Mrs Tower's behaviour wonderful?
11 Why was it the most amusing meal that Somerset Maugham had ever attended?
12 Mrs Tower was so angry that for once she told the truth.
  (a) What did she say that was true?
  (b) What does this sentence tell us about Mrs Tower's character?
  (c) What was the difference in ages between Jane Fowler and Gilbert Napier?
13 I really had to laugh and Gilbert laughed too.
  (a) What remark did Jane Fowler make which they both found so funny?
  (b) What was Gilbert amused by?
  (c) Was Mrs Tower amused?
14 'You see he has never had more than a fortnight's holiday before,' Jane Fowler told them.
  (a) Why had Gilbert never had more than a fortnight's holiday before?
  (b) What exclamation did Mrs Tower make?
  (c) What did she mean by the exclamation?
15 'Why are you marrying this young man?' Mrs Tower asked Jane Fowler.
  (a) What was Jane Fowler's reply?
  (b) What did Mrs Tower say was the real reason that Gilbert Napier was marrying Jane Fowler?
16 'I would never have believed that you would fall in love with a boy,' said Mrs Tower.
  (a) Was Jane Fowler in love with Gilbert Napier?
  (b) Why did Jane Fowler want to marry the young man?
  (c) Why had she never married a man of her own age?

17 What agreement about divorce had Jane Fowler and Gilbert made between them?
18 Mrs Tower now made a cruel remark.
   (a) What cruel remark did she make?
   (b) What was Jane Fowler's reply to this remark?
19 How long did Mrs Tower think the marriage would last?
20 'Are you sure she's dull?' I said.
   (a) Did Somerset Maugham think that she was really dull?
   (b) What was Mrs Tower's reply?
21 Somerset Maugham heard nothing more about this strange marriage for two years.
   (a) Why had he heard nothing about the marriage?
   (b) Where was he when he met Mrs Tower again?
22 Somerset Maugham asked Mrs Tower if she had seen much of Jane and Gilbert Napier.
   (a) What was her reply?
   (b) What had happened to Jane?
   (c) Who was at the same dinner party?
23 Our hostess was a bright and amusing woman.
   (a) Why was Somerset Maugham sure that his hostess would not invite Jane to her dinner party?
   (b) Why had Somerset Maugham noticed the woman who was sitting next to the host?
   (c) Why had he not recognised Jane at first?
24 At that moment Mrs Napier was speaking to the host.
   (a) What happened when Jane finished speaking?
   (b) What did the famous politician say to Mrs Tower?
25 Mrs Tower told me the story.
   (a) What happened when Jane changed her style of clothes?
   (b) How had Gilbert and Jane stopped other people wearing the same dresses as she did?
26 Sir Reginald Frobisher seemed to be always at the same parties she went to.
   (a) Why was Sir Reginald Frobisher an important person?
   (b) What did he think of Jane's amusing conversation?
27 Even Mrs Tower agreed that she had been wrong about Gilbert.
   (a) How did her attitude to Gilbert change?
   (b) How long did she think the marriage would last?

28 'Jane and Gilbert have parted,' Mrs Tower told Maugham.
    (a) What agreement had Jane and Gilbert made before they got married?
    (b) What did Somerset Maugham think had happened?
    (c) What had really happened?
29 The door opened and the butler announced the arrival of Jane.
    (a) What did Jane ask Mrs Tower to do?
    (b) What had Mrs Tower once advised Jane to do?
    (c) What had Gilbert promised to go on doing?
30 Why did Jane think she had been married to Gilbert long enough?
31 What was Jane planning to do for Gilbert?
32 She gave us a strange look through her eyeglass. I knew it would upset Mrs Tower, but I had to laugh.
    (a) What had Jane just said which made Somerset Maugham laugh?
    (b) Did Jane think herself an amusing person?
    (c) What did Jane think was the reason for people finding her amusing?
33 'But why am I the only person who does not think it funny?' asked Mrs Tower.
    (a) What did Jane say in reply to this question?
    (b) Why did Somerset Maugham think Jane was wonderful?

Glossary

SECTION 1

Terms to do with literature and writing books

critic (page 4)
> a person who reads books and writes his or her opinion of them in a newspaper.

learned (page 4)
> pronounced learnèd, with the stress on the last syllable. Used here as an adjective meaning full of learning – often meaning books which are not easy to read.

merit – *literary merit* (page 4)
> a writer of literary merit is one who is recognised by the critics as a very good writer – a writer who uses words skilfully. If the critics and the public like a writer's books he or she may get a literary reputation. The person will be known as an important writer. A writer may have literary merit, but his or her books may not be liked by the public, who may think they are too difficult.

public (page 4)
> ordinary people – here contrasted with critics.

quote (page 6)
> to repeat from memory something you have read or heard.

SECTION 2

Terms to do with polite society

These three short stories are set in England in the 1920s. At that time, people who were in polite society were upper-class people who were usually wealthy. They had servants who did all the housework and so people in polite society had plenty of time to meet each other for tea-parties and dinner-parties. In London, people in polite society all knew each other and invited each other to their houses.

attitudes – *beliefs and attitudes* (page 28)
> people in polite society believed in the same things and thought in the same way about things. Sometimes these beliefs and attitudes changed, but Mr and Mrs St Clair were old-fashioned and had not changed. See *fashionable* below.

Bulfinch (page 15)

ladies and gentlemen in polite society were always given their full titles (Mr or Mrs) when spoken to. In this story, for example, Somerset Maugham always speaks about *Mrs* Albert Forrester. But a cook was not a lady and so when Mrs Albert Forrester speaks to her, she uses her surname only – Bulfinch.

butler (page 42)

a manservant in an upper-class house. The butler was in charge of the other servants and made sure they did their work properly. He also introduced guests when they came into the drawing-room.

charwoman (page 42)

a woman who worked as a cleaner in the houses of upper-class people. The word is now considered impolite and a person who does cleaning for other people is called a 'cleaning lady'.

dignity (page 15)

Mrs Albert Forrester speaks with dignity, calmly and seriously, when she addresses Mrs Bulfinch. She is a member of polite society and she speaks to her servant without calling her *Mrs*. Mrs Forrester expects to be treated with proper respect.

drawing-room (page 5)

a large room in a house where guests sit and are offered tea while they talk to each other.

fashionable (page 5)

the people who were in polite society followed certain rules about how to dress and how to behave. They followed the fashion. Some parts of London were thought to be more fashionable than others, so people in polite society bought houses in those parts. Fashions often change and something which was considered fashionable at one time might be considered old-fashioned at a later date. Some people, as they grow older, refuse to change their habits: they keep to the fashion of many years ago.

girl – *old girl* (page 17)

an affectionate, loving way working-class men speak to their wives. People in polite society did not speak to each other using this expression.

honoured (page 6)

the honoured guest at a party was usually an important person whom everybody wanted to meet.

hostess/host (page 51)
> the hostess or host at a party is the person giving the party to which their friends are invited as guests.

improper (page 28)
> not polite. Mr and Mrs St Clair thought that certain books were improper and should not be read by young ladies who were in polite society.

old-fashioned (page 24)
> see *fashionable* above.

party – fancy-dress party (page 51)
> a party where the guests wear unusual clothes. For example, the guests come dressed in clothes that were fashionable many, many years ago.

porter (page 9)
> a man who earned money by carrying goods from one place to another. For example, from a shop to a person's house. Today, the word porter is used for a person who works in a railway station or a hotel.

references (page 10)
> when a servant left one job to go to another, their employer gave them a paper saying how they did their work and how they behaved.

reputation – destroy your reputation (page 13)
> the public believe that Mrs Forrester is a writer of literary merit (See Section One, above) and that she is happily married to a good, kind man. If the public finds out that Mr Forrester has gone to live with a servant, they will think that Mrs Forrester has done something wrong. They might also stop buying her books because they believe Mr and Mrs Forrester have behaved badly. Mrs Forrester's reputation will be destroyed.

respectable-looking – a respectable-looking, middle-aged, well-dressed gentleman (page 19)
> the clothes the gentleman was wearing showed that he was a man in polite society. He was not a workman. A respectable person is a middle-class or upper-class person who is in polite society.

scandal (page 14)
> if something shameful happened in polite society, everyone talked about it. It was a scandal.

serve (page 5)

in polite society, guests sat in the drawing-room or at table and the servants served the tea or the food – brought the tea or food to them. At Mrs Albert Forrester's afternoon tea-parties, the tea was served not by a servant, but by Miss Warren.

society – *London society* (page 13)

see the note on polite society at the beginning of this section. See also *fashionable* above.

SECTION 3

Terms describing emotions and emotional reactions

The heart was at one time thought to be where we felt emotions. There are many phrases describing emotions which have the word heart in them.

blush (page 29)

a redness in the cheeks which shows that a person is embarrassed or ashamed.

curious (page 27)

wanting to know more about something.

desperate (page 17)

not knowing what to do in a difficult situation.

dismay – *gasp of dismay* (page 10)

a short, sharp breath which we make when we suddenly hear very bad news.

distress (page 37)

to be in distress is to be very unhappy because you are in great trouble.

embarrass (page 10)

to be embarrassed is not knowing what to do or say when something, possibly shameful, happens in front of other people.

envy (page 6)

upset or sad because someone else has something which you would like to have.

frown (page 8)

to frown is to bring together your eyebrows. The lines on your forehead show that you are angry or upset.

gold – *heart of gold* (page 42)

see the note on the word *heart* at the beginning of this section. A person who has a heart of gold is a very honest and very good person.

heart – *bitterness in her heart* (page 55)

see the note on the word *heart* at the beginning of this section. Mrs Tower felt very upset and envied Jane Napier's success.

heart – *broke her heart* (page 36)

see the note on the word *heart* at the beginning of this section. Made her so sad that she was never able to be happy again in her life.

heart – *spoke from her heart* (page 56)

see the note on the word *heart* at the beginning of this section. Jane Napier spoke the truth without trying to make what she was saying sound better.

heartless (page 58)

a cruel person.

melancholy (page 27)

something which makes you feel very sad and gloomy.

puzzling (page 41)

difficult to understand – confusing.

respect (page 8)

to respect someone is to think highly of them.

sank – *my heart sank* (page 23)

see the note on the word *heart* at the beginning of this section. The writer suddenly felt sad and unhappy.

sigh (page 27)

to breathe out and make a soft noise which shows you are sad or unhappy about something.

SECTION 4

Terms to do with marriage

back – *to get someone back, to take someone back* (page 12)

both these phrases refer to a marriage in which one partner has left the other. To get someone back is to *persuade* the other partner to come back. (See *persuade* in Section Five, below.) To take someone back is to *allow* the other partner to come back. Mr Simmons is trying to tell Mrs Albert Forrester that her husband has left her and she must persuade him to come back.

bigamist (page 30)

in English law, a man is only allowed to marry one wife. A man who marries another woman while he has a wife is committing a crime. The crime is called bigamy and the criminal is a bigamist.

divorce (page 10)

a legal arrangement to end a marriage.

elope (page 10)

the law in England in the 1920s did not allow a woman under twenty-one years of age to marry without her parents' approval. A young woman who ran away from her parents in order to get married, eloped. Also, anyone who runs away secretly to get married is said to have eloped.

spinster (page 31)

a woman who has never married.

SECTION 5

General

Admiral-of-the-Fleet (page 55)

an important officer in the British navy.

architect (page 43)

a person who makes drawings of buildings – designs them so that a builder can build them.

book – *a visitor's book* (page 24)

a book kept in boarding houses where the visitors must write down their names and addresses.

bow (page 27)

a polite way of greeting someone by bending the body from the waist. No longer used as a way of greeting a person, except in a court or in church ceremonies.

City – *the City of London* (page 6)

the part of London where banks and businesses dealing with money have their headquarters.

clergyman (page 33)

a priest or a minister in a Christian church.

cuttings – *newspaper cuttings* (page 31)

a piece cut out from a newspaper which refers to something of interest to the person who cut it out.

design (page 54)

to design a dress is to make a drawing of it so that a tailor can use the design to make the dress.

dozen (page 4)

a group of twelve things. See the examples of phrases with the word *dozen* in them in paragraph 4, on page 4.

ears – *could not believe my ears* (page 43)

an expression to describe something you hear that is so strange that you cannot believe it.

embroidery (page 24)

a special way of stitching with coloured threads to make pretty patterns on cloth. Young ladies were encouraged to do embroidery or knitting (see below) in their spare time.

graceful (page 24)

the lady stood and walked in a pleasing way.

grave – *one foot in the grave* (page 44)

a person who has one foot in the grave is so old or so ill that they are almost dead.

house – *boarding house* (page 23)

a house where visitors pay money to stay – a small hotel.

influenza (page 23)

an illness which is similar to a cold, but more serious. In the 1920s, many people died from influenza.

knitting (page 24)

using needles and wool to make clothes. See *embroidery* above.

manufacturer (page 42)

the owner of a factory which produces goods.

merchant – *currant merchant* (page 7)

a merchant in the City of London buys and sells goods often imported from abroad. A City merchant does not actually see the goods – all the buying and selling is done by letter or by telephone. Mr Forrester buys and sells currants – dried fruit.

persuade (page 17)

to talk to someone and try to get them to do what you want.

poverty – *in poverty* (page 13)

poverty is the noun from the adjective 'poor'. To live in poverty is to have very little money.

seafront (page 23)

the part of a seaside town where people can walk or sit down and look out at the sea.

shabby (page 15)

   a shabby house is a house which has not been cared for and needs
   cleaning and painting.

solicitor (page 19)

   someone trained in the law. A solicitor looks after other people's
   private business and so learns a lot about a person's private life.

subdued (page 41)

   the opposite of bright.

tram (page 14)

   a tram is like a bus and takes passengers round a town or city.
   The tram runs along on rails in the street (like a train) and is
   driven by electricity.

unique (page 54)

   a thing which is unique is the only one of its kind. There is no
   other one the same.

W. SOMERSET MAUGHAM
unsimplified

FICTION

Liza of Lambeth
Mrs Craddock
The Magician
Of Human Bondage
The Moon and Sixpence
The Trembling of a Leaf
On a Chinese Screen
The Painted Veil
The Casuarina Tree
Ashenden
The Gentleman in the Parlour
Cakes and Ale
First Person Singular
The Narrow Corner

Ah King
Don Fernando
Cosmopolitans
Theatre
The Summing Up
Christmas Holiday
Books and You
The Mixture as Before
Up at the Villa
Strictly Personal
The Razor's Edge
Then and Now
Creatures of Circumstance
Catalina

Here and There (*Collection of Short Stories*)
Quartet (*Four Short Stories with Film Scripts*)
A Writer's Notebook
Trio (*Three Short Stories with Film Scripts*)
The Complete Short Stories (3 *Vols.*)
Encore (*Three Short Stories with Film Scripts*)
The Vagrant Mood
The Collected Plays (3 *Vols.*)
The Selected Novels (3 *Vols.*)
The Partial View
Ten Novels and Their Authors
The Travel Books

Of Mice and Men *by John Steinbeck*
Bleak House *by Charles Dickens*
The Great Ponds *by Elechi Amadi*
Rebecca *by Daphne du Maurier*
Our Mutual Friend *by Charles Dickens*
The Grapes of Wrath *by John Steinbeck*
The Return of the Native *by Thomas Hardy*
Weep Not, Child *by Ngũgĩ wa Thiong'o*
Precious Bane *by Mary Webb*
Mine Boy *by Peter Abrahams*

For further information on the full selection of Readers
at all five levels in the series, please refer to the
Heinemann Guided Readers catalogue.

Heinemann English Language Teaching
A division of Heinemann Publishers (Oxford) Ltd
Halley Court, Jordan Hill, Oxford OX2 8EJ

OXFORD MADRID ATHENS PARIS FLORENCE PRAGUE
SÃO PAULO CHICAGO MELBOURNE AUCKLAND
SINGAPORE TOKYO GABORONE
JOHANNESBURG PORTSMOUTH (NH) IBADAN

ISBN 0 435 27262 4

The Creative Impulse was first published by William Heinemann Ltd in 1926,
The Round Dozen in 1924 and *Jane* in 1923,
and are included in the
Complete Short Stories of W. Somerset Maugham (Volume Two).
These retold versions for Heinemann Guided Readers
© John Milne 1987, 1992
First published 1987
Reprinted twice
This edition published 1992

Illustrated by Paul Sullivan
Typography by Adrian Hodgkins
Cover by Janet Woolley and Threefold Design
Typeset in 10.5/12.5 pt Goudy
by Joshua Associates Ltd, Oxford
Printed and bound in Malta by Interprint Limited

93 94 95 96 97 10 9 8 7 6 5 4 3